Words MATTER

FAMILY

Book One

Written by Jacob Paul Patchen
Illustrated by Cody Willoughby

ART SQUAD
NETTLETON
STEAM

PARTNERSHIP

T P
P

Relax. Read. Repeat.

MW00890380

FAMILY (WORDS THAT MATTER, BOOK 1)
Published by TouchPoint Press
Brookland, Arkansas 72417
www.touchpointpress.com

Copyright © 2021 Jacob Paul Patchen
Cover Design: Colbie Myles
Interior Design: David Ter-Avanesyan/Ter33Design
Cover Illustrations: Cody Willoughby, Nettleton STEAM Art Teacher and
creator of the Nettleton STEAM Art Squad

PRINT ISBN-13: 978-1-952816-29-1

First Edition

Printed in the United States of America.

For my family, who taught me to love
through actions, care through support, and to laugh
everything else away.

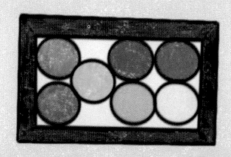

"Come along now kids, it's story time."
Grandpa Goose waddled over to
his old rocking chair and sat
down. He wiggled and he
jiggled until he was as
comfortable and as
snug as a mouse in
a mouse house.

One by one, the kids
hurried into the living room.

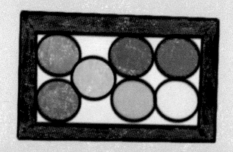

Tuffy Goose came marching in first. His boots made a heavy thud on the living room floor.

"Left, left, left-right, left," he said, as he came to a stop in front of Grandpa. He raised a wing and saluted. "Tuffy Goose reporting for duty, SIR!"

Grandpa laughed. "10-4."

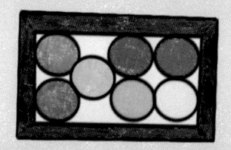

Next was Lovey Goose.
She came skipping into
the living room with a
pink bow in her hair.
She skipped over to
Grandpa Goose
and gave him
a kiss on
the cheek.

"I love
story time,"
she said, smiling.
"And I love you too,
Grandpa."

"You're so sweet," he said.

"Where's Silly Goose?"
Grandpa Goose asked.

Tuffy Goose and Lovey
Goose looked at each
other and shrugged.

A loud BANG
came from
the hallway.

Silly Goose
tumbled into the
living room with
his orange t-shirt
over his head.

"What on Earth?"
Grandma Goose said,
sticking her head out
from the kitchen.

"Oh, Silly Goose,
what have you gotten
into this time?"
Grandpa Goose asked.

"I think I got it."
Silly Goose laughed,
sticking his head out of
the shirt's arm hole.

"Ohhh, Silly Gooose."
they all said.

Grandpa, Grandma, Tuffy, Lovey, and Silly Goose sat in the living room ready for Grandpa's story.

Once upon a time, he started, there was a family of fish that lived in the sea.

Grandpa paused. "Who can tell me what a family is?"

"Ooo Ooo, I know, I know."
Silly Goose had his wing waving wildly in the air.

"Go ahead." Grandpa encouraged.

Silly Goose looked around the room nervously.
"Family is . . . the sofa . . . the lamp . . . the rug . . .
the coffee table. . . ."

"Ohhh, Silly Gooose!" Grandma laughed. "A family is those you care most about. Like your brother, your sister, your mom and dad. And even us, your old grandparents.

"That's right," Grandpa agreed. "Family is everyone you are related to. Even your aunts, uncles and cousins."

"And sometimes, a family can be everyone who lives together," Grandma added.

Grandpa Goose continued his story.

It was a family of fish. There was Mother Fish, Father Fish, Kid Fish, Baby Sister, Grandma, Grandpa, Aunts, Uncles and Cousins. There was even a stepfather, a stepmother, a stepsister, and a stepbrother.

Every holiday and birthday party, the whole family would come together. It was always so exciting to see everyone, but it was a large family and a small house.

Kid Fish was about to
turn seven years old.

"I can't wait to open all of my
birthday presents,"
he told Mother.

Kid Fish thought about how much fun he had playing with his cousins. They would play tag in the yard, hide and go seek in the house, and they would go exploring outside.

Kid fish felt bad about only thinking about his presents.
"I'm excited to play with my cousins!"

The whole family came to celebrate Kid Fish's birthday. Kid Fish got lots of hugs and kisses.

There was so much laughter and talking. Father talked about his job down at the water plant, Grandma talked about her new coconut pie, and Grandpa talked about his pet seahorses.

"That's not fair!" she said. Baby Sister started to cry.

"If you're going to be a cry baby, then go inside." Kid Fish said.

Father heard Kid Fish. He crossed his fins and looked sternly at the children. "Kid Fish! That is no way to treat your Baby Sister. You should apologize and tell her you love her."

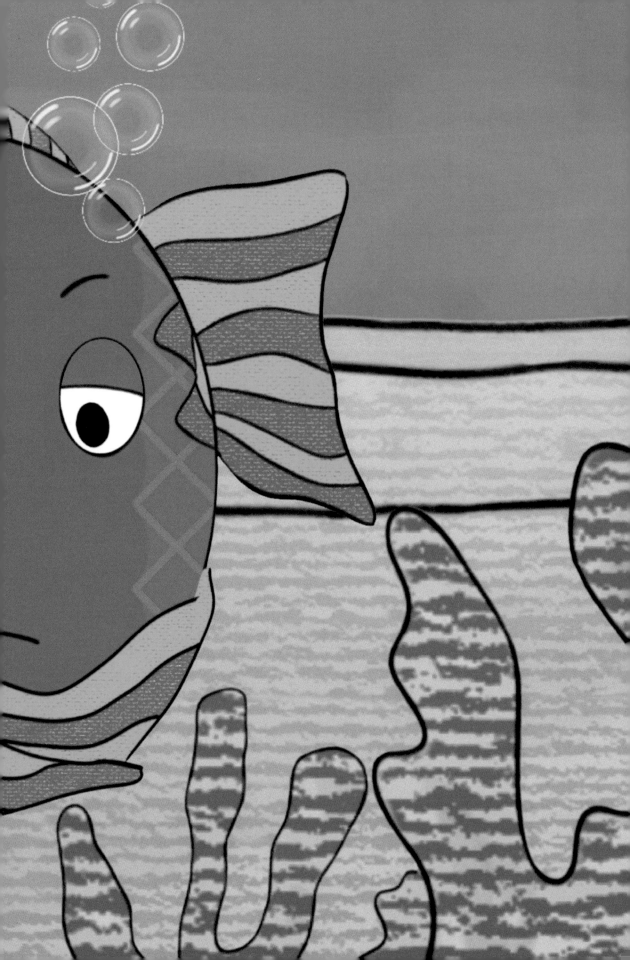

Kid Fish was ashamed. He hung his
head and looked sadly at the ground.
"I'm sorry Baby Sister. It wasn't right
for me to do that. I love you and
I should be nice to you.
After all, you're my family.
I should protect you,
not hurt your feelings."

He hugged Baby Sister and wiped away the last of her tears.

It was time for Kid Fish
to open his presents.
He got a new ball, a
new bat. And a new hat.

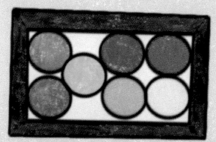

Silly Goose couldn't hold in his excitement. "What is it, Grandpa?"

"Silly Goose," Grandpa laughed, "you have to be patient."

Grandpa continued his story.

"It's a
FIIIRE TRUUUUCK!"
Kid Fish squealed.

It had lights, a ladder, a fire hose, and a
fireman. It even made noises and beeped its
horn. Woo-woo. Beep. Beep. Kid Fish loved
his new toy and he played with it all day.

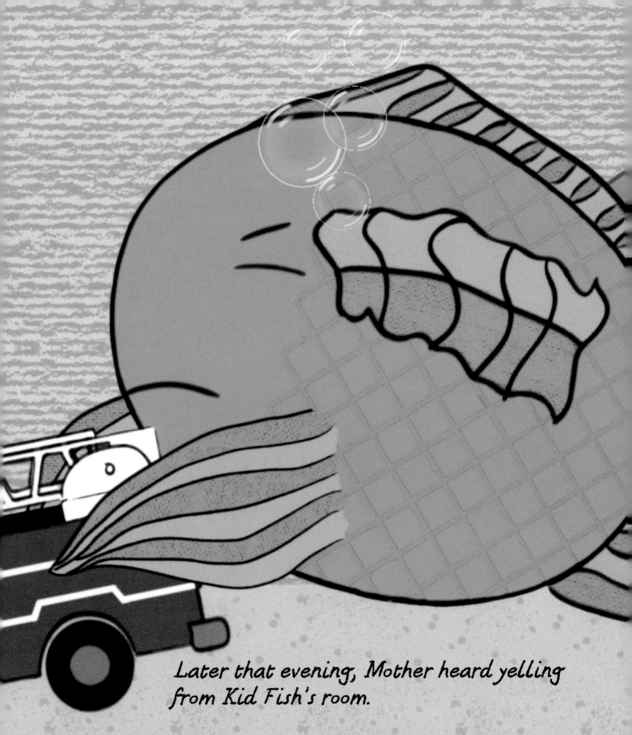

Later that evening, Mother heard yelling
from Kid Fish's room.

"Stop! You're going to break it!" Kid Fish yelled.

"What's going on?" Mother demanded.

"Baby Sister won't stop playing with my fire truck,"
he whined, stomping his flipper.

"Kid Fish, you need to share with your sister," Mother scolded.

"But why? It's my favorite toy!"

"You share because she is your family and families share with one another," Mother explained.

Just then, the wheel on
the fire truck broke.

"Oh No!" cried Kid fish.
"Now it's broken."

"I'm sorry," Baby Sister
said sadly, her eyes wide.

Baby Sister ran into her room and grabbed her favorite doll. She tore off one of the buttons and hurried back to Kid Fish and Mother.

"Here big brother, you can use this for a wheel." She offered the button to him.

The button fit onto the fire truck.

"It works!" Kid Fish shouted.

"See," said Mother proudly, "
families help one another."

From then on, Kid Fish shared his toys with Baby Sister.

The End, Grandpa Goose finished.

"Why do you think
Baby Sister broke her
toy to fix Kid Fish's
fire truck?"
Grandma asked.

Tuffy Goose smirked.
"So she could play with it."

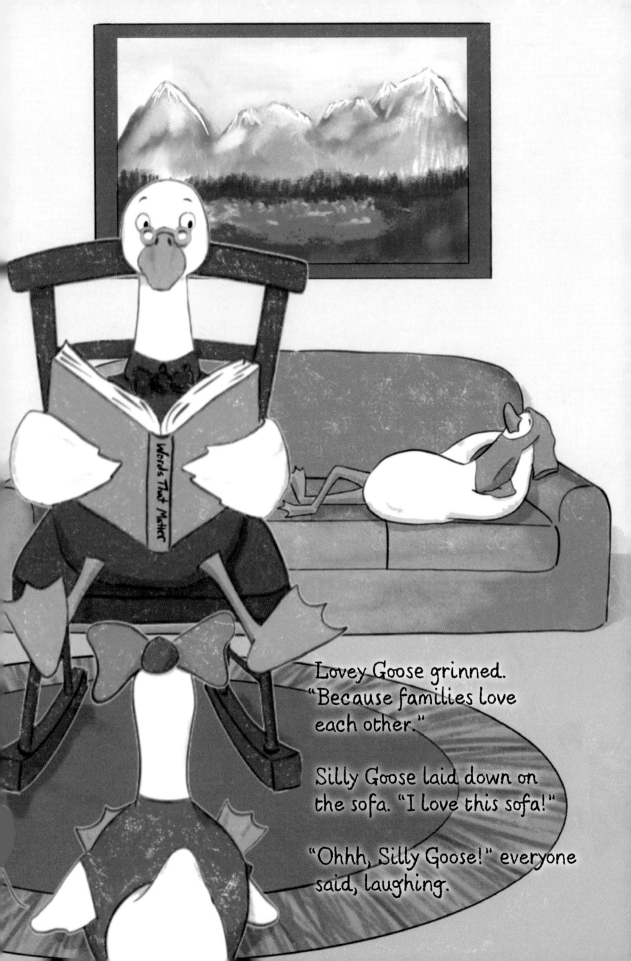

Lovey Goose grinned. "Because families love each other."

Silly Goose laid down on the sofa. "I love this sofa!"

"Ohhh, Silly Goose!" everyone said, laughing.

ABOUT THE AUTHOR

Jacob Paul Patchen grew up outside of Byesville, Ohio where spent his youth tormenting babysitters and hiding in trees. Jacob earns his inspiration through experience, while using wit and grit to write about family, love, humor, learning, and war. Jacob is an author, poet, blogger, and combat veteran. Patchen debuted with his 5-star book, *Life Lesson's from Grandpa and His Chicken Coop* (2015). He is a published poet, contest finalist, and author of a full-length poetry book, *Of Love and War* (Adelaide Books, 2018).

Family is the first of ten titles in the Words That Matter children's picture book series.

ABOUT THE ILLUSTRATOR

Art has been a passion of mine since I was very little. I spent many years as a martial arts instructor, which is where I discovered my passion for teaching. Once I saw the strong connection between art and learning, I knew I wanted to be an art teacher. I got my Bachelor's Degree in Art Education at Arkansas State University in 2018 and went on to teach art at Nettleton STEAM, where I devote my time to integrating the arts into STEM education.

ABOUT THE ART SQUAD

The Art Squad is a small group of dedicated 5th and 6th grade artists at Nettleton STEAM. Their mission is to take on projects that help to serve others using their artistic skills and expertise. They started illustrating the first book of the Words That Matter series "Family" by Jacob Paul Patchen, in the Fall of 2019 with the assistance of their art teacher Cody Willoughby. The Art Squad will be illustrating future books in the Words That Matter series as part of their mission to help others through art.

Art Squad Teacher:

Cody Willoughby

Art Squad Members:

Jocelyn L.
Katelyn R.
Reagan N.
Caden C.
Hunter T.
Grayson P.
Lily B.
Sky R.
Layla W.
Destinee F.
Abbie B.
Raegan S.

FOR PARENTS AND TEACHERS

Words matter. But understanding them matters even more. *The Words That Matter* series delivers meaning, understanding, and enjoyment to the whole family.

The series is written with children around the ages of 3 to 7 in mind, but families, teachers, schools, guardians, mothers, fathers, and grandparents will enjoy the entertaining stories and chance to engage in open communication with the child/children in their lives.

EDUCATIONAL, LIBRARY
AND GROUP REQUESTS

If you would like more information on purchasing *Family* (*Words That Matter, Book 1*) for your classroom, school library, or group, contact:

TouchPoint Press
General email: info@touchpointpress.com
Review and interview requests: media@touchpointpress.com
Visit us online: www.touchpointpress.com
General inquiries: 662-595-4162
Fax: 870-200-6702

Made in the USA
Monee, IL
11 May 2021